Dear Parents and Educators,

Welcome to Penguin Young Readers! As parents and educators, you know that each child develops at his or her own pace—in terms of speech, critical thinking, and, of course, reading. Penguin Young Readers recognizes this fact. As a result, each Penguin Young Readers book is assigned a traditional easy-to-read level (1–4) as well as a Guided Reading Level (A–P). Both of these systems will help you choose the right book for your child. Please refer to the back of each book for specific leveling information. Penguin Young Readers features esteemed authors and illustrators, stories about favorite characters, fascinating nonfiction, and more!

Pajama Party

LEVEL 2

GUIDED READING LEVEL **E**

This book is perfect for a **Progressing Reader** who:
- can figure out unknown words by using picture and context clues;
- can recognize beginning, middle, and ending sounds;
- can make and confirm predictions about what will happen in the text; and
- can distinguish between fiction and nonfiction.

Here are some **activities** you can do during and after reading this book:
- Rhyming Words: On a separate piece of paper, make a list of all the rhyming words in this story. For example, *eat* rhymes with *treat*, so write those two words next to each other.
- Make Connections: Have you ever been to a pajama party? What did you do at your party that was the same as what the girls in this story do? What did you do that was different?

Remember, sharing the love of reading with a child is the best gift you can give!

—Bonnie Bader, EdM
  Penguin Young Readers program

*Penguin Young Readers are leveled by independent reviewers applying the standards developed by Irene Fountas and Gay Su Pinnell in *Matching Books to Readers: Using Leveled Books in Guided Reading*, Heinemann, 1999.

For Karen Kershner Slack,
a good friend—JH

For my niece, Katie—JD

Penguin Young Readers
Published by the Penguin Group
Penguin Group (USA) Inc., 375 Hudson Street, New York, New York 10014, USA
Penguin Group (Canada), 90 Eglinton Avenue East, Suite 700, Toronto, Ontario M4P 2Y3, Canada
(a division of Pearson Penguin Canada Inc.)
Penguin Books Ltd., 80 Strand, London WC2R 0RL, England
Penguin Group Ireland, 25 St. Stephen's Green, Dublin 2, Ireland (a division of Penguin Books Ltd.)
Penguin Group (Australia), 250 Camberwell Road, Camberwell, Victoria 3124, Australia
(a division of Pearson Australia Group Pty. Ltd.)
Penguin Books India Pvt. Ltd., 11 Community Centre, Panchsheel Park, New Delhi—110 017, India
Penguin Group (NZ), 67 Apollo Drive, Rosedale, Auckland 0632, New Zealand
(a division of Pearson New Zealand Ltd.)
Penguin Books (South Africa) (Pty.) Ltd., 24 Sturdee Avenue,
Rosebank, Johannesburg 2196, South Africa

Penguin Books Ltd., Registered Offices: 80 Strand, London WC2R 0RL, England

Library of Congress Control Number: 97039734

ISBN 978-0-448-41739-4   10 9 8 7 6 5 4

Pajama Party

by Joan Holub
illustrated by Julie Durrell

Penguin Young Readers
An Imprint of Penguin Group (USA) Inc.

Tonight is my pajama party.

I can hardly wait.

My friends are coming over.

And we plan to stay up late.

Ding-dong!

Look who's here!

It's Meg and Jen and Dee.

Keesha's here, and Emma, too.

That makes six, with me.

Mmmm . . .

The pizza's ready now.

Quick!

Let's go and eat!

After that, banana splits

make a yummy treat.

The sky is black.

The moon is bright.

And all the stars are out.

It's party time—let's boogie!

We sing!

We dance!

We shout!

No one wants to go to bed.

Let's stay up all night instead!

We paint our nails with polish—

all sparkly blue and green.

Then we fix each other's hair.

Jen looks like a queen.

Dee passes out some bubble gum.

Then she blows a bubble.

We can't believe how big it is!

Uh-oh.

Bubble trouble.

No one wants to go to bed.

Let's stay up all night instead.

Emma starts a pillow fight.

We whack and whomp each other.

Pillows zoom across the room.

Oops! I got my mother!

We munch on chips and popcorn
while a movie plays.

Then we get our bedrolls out
and put on our pj's.

But no one wants to go to bed.

Let's stay up all night instead.

Emma gets the hiccups.

Keesha gets the wiggles.

Jen, Meg, and Dee tell jokes.

And me? I get the giggles!

Next we all share secrets
and tell ghost stories, too.

I put on a big,
white sheet.
Look out!
I'm coming!
Boo!

Now we snuggle in our bedrolls

and hug our pillows tight.

We must not close our eyes because
we **must** stay up all night!

But Keesha yawns and

stretches out.

Dee doesn't make a peep.

Meg and Emma rub their eyes.

And Jen falls fast asleep.

Everybody's snoozing now.

Everyone but me.

I'm not sleepy—not at all.

It's only half past three.

I close my eyes a minute,

just to take a break.

It may look like I'm sleeping,

but . . .

. . . I'm not—I'm wide awake!